The story of
Carl Pug

Joëlle Tourlonias studied Visual Communication at the Bauhaus University of Weimar, specialising in Illustrating and Painting. She has published various picture books. Her first children's book was published by Jacoby & Stuart and was nominated for the French/German Award for Youth Literature 2015.

Fabiola Nonn studied at the Art Academy of Stuttgart and at the College for Art therapy of Nürtingen.

Lukas Weidenbach was trained as a bookshop owner and then studied Media and Cultural Sciences. He now works for a publishing house in Frankfurt.

Translation: Marion Singor
Typesetting: Teo van Gerwen

www.aerialmediacom.nl
www.facebook.com/Aerialmediacompany

ISBN 978-94-026-0138-1

Aerial Media Company bv. Postbus 6088, 4000 HB Tiel, The Netherlands

Fabiola Nonn Lukas Weidenbach Joëlle Tourlonias

A new adventure of
Carl Pug

Carl falls madly in love and finds a girlfriend

Aerial Media Company

My name is Carl and I'm a pug. Today's a lovely day and I'm out for a walk in the city with my owner and my best friend, Paula. Suddenly – oh, who is that? She is the most beautiful girl dog I have ever seen! Suddenly my heart begins hammering in my chest.

Back home, I can't sleep. My tummy is fluttering as if I've swallowed a butterfly. Paula is watching me, and finally says, "Hey, what's wrong, little pug?" "Oh Paula," I sigh. "I can't stop thinking about that beautiful girl dog we saw. Her ears were so fluffy and she smelled better than any bone, didn't she?" "Ah, I know what's wrong with you," laughs Paula. "You're in love! Lucky you!"

Early next morning we are woken by shouts outside. We look out of the
window, and see – of all people – the pretty girl dog's master. He's yelling,
"Coco! Coco, where are you?" Ah, so she's called Coco – what an adorable name.
But, dear me, she seems to be lost.

"Paula, my lovely Coco is lost!" I shout. "She's out there somewhere, all alone.
She must be so scared. We have to find her!" "Oh, all right," sighs Paula. "But
we'd better be back before our owner gets home, or we'll be in big trouble."
Paula jumps through the window into the garden – I knew she would help.

We search for hours, but Coco is nowhere to be found. At the canal, we bump into the
big friendly dog Peter. He has lived here for years and everyone knows he's the best
in town at tracking scents. Breathlessly, I tell him all about our search for Coco and
what she looks like – a beautiful dog with fluffy ears, who smells divine.
"I've seen her!" says Peter straight away, sniffing down the canal bank with his snout.
"Come on – I'm sure we'll find her," he says, rushing off on Coco's trail.

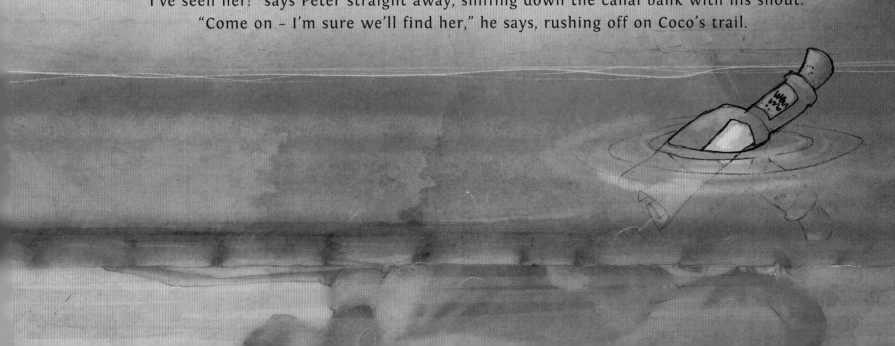

Before long we reach a tunnel and stop. "It's really dark in there," I shudder. Suddenly, a frightened whimper comes from inside the tunnel. "Coco?" I whisper. Then we hear a loud bark and a snarl, and we can smell bad breath and dirty fur – my Coco's in danger. "Quick!" I shout. I muster all my courage and start to run.

Sure enough, inside the tunnel, we find Coco, surrounded by a gang of nasty dogs. Small as I am, I must save her, so I bark as loud as I can and shout, "Leave her alone!" The eyes of the other dogs glitter dangerously and the biggest one growls, "This is our territory." I can't help being scared, but Paula and Peter are right by my side.

"Harm one hair on Coco's head and you'll have us to deal with,"
snarls Paula, and she begins to bark. Peter and I join in. Together
we are so loud that the street dogs are taken aback. In the end,
their leader shrugs and says, "I'm getting bored with this.
Let's leave, boys." They slink off.

"Phew, that was close," says Coco. "Thank you!" Her voice is so pretty it makes me feel all warm and fuzzy. "How on earth did you end up here?" asks Paula. "I was chasing butterflies and suddenly I didn't know where I was," Coco explains. "Then that gang of bad dogs showed up and...oh, I'm so happy you found me."

Suddenly I hear another loud snarl, which makes me flinch.
"No, it's okay – that was my tummy rumbling!" laughs Coco.
I realise now that I'm hungry too. "Let's go to the market
place," suggests Coco. "There's always something to eat there.
But how do we find the way?"

"No worries – I know the way!" chorus Peter and Paula, and
then look at each other in surprise.

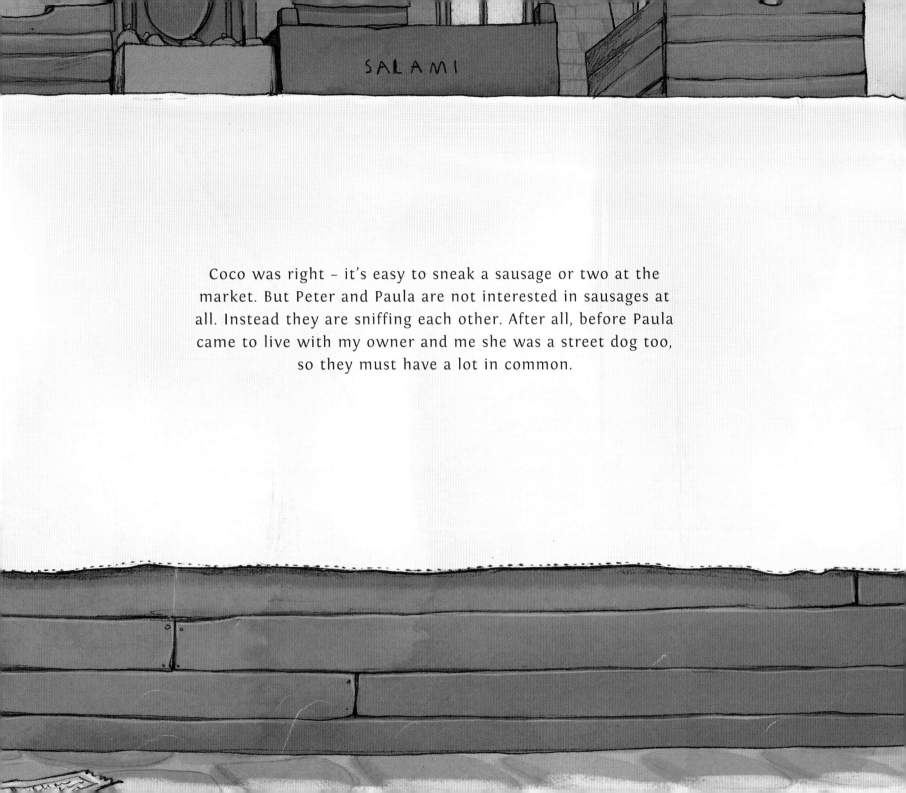

Coco was right – it's easy to sneak a sausage or two at the market. But Peter and Paula are not interested in sausages at all. Instead they are sniffing each other. After all, before Paula came to live with my owner and me she was a street dog too, so they must have a lot in common.

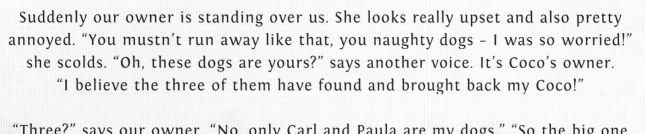

Suddenly our owner is standing over us. She looks really upset and also pretty annoyed. "You mustn't run away like that, you naughty dogs – I was so worried!" she scolds. "Oh, these dogs are yours?" says another voice. It's Coco's owner. "I believe the three of them have found and brought back my Coco!"

"Three?" says our owner. "No, only Carl and Paula are my dogs." "So the big one isn't yours?" says Coco's owner. "He seems to get along very well with Paula." "You're right, he does," says our owner, who seems to have forgotten she is mad with us. In fact she seems to be a bit proud of our bravery now. And me? I'm just so happy we found Coco. I think I'm in love.